I0692489

Anonymous

The Life of Archbishop Hughes, First Archbishop of New York

with a full account of his life, death and burial as well as his services in all

pursuits and vocations from his birth until his death

Anonymous

The Life of Archbishop Hughes, First Archbishop of New York
*with a full account of his life, death and burial as well as his services in all pursuits
and vocations from his birth until his death*

ISBN/EAN: 9783337388171

Printed in Europe, USA, Canada, Australia, Japan

Cover: Foto ©Andreas Hilbeck / pixelio.de

More available books at **www.hansebooks.com**

ARCHBISHOP HUGHES.

(FIRST ARCHBISHOP OF NEW YORK.)

With a full account of his Life, Death, and Burial; as well as his
Services in all pursuits and vocations, from his
Birth until his Death.

BORN IN CLOGHER, IRELAND, 1798.
DIED IN NEW YORK, JAN 3, 1864.

"BURY ME IN THE SUNSHINE."

Archbishop Hughes' last words.

.

"I have fought the good fight; I have finished the course, I have kept the
faith; for the rest I know there is laid up for me a crown of justice, which the
Just Judge shall render to me."—*Funeral Oration of Bishop McCloskey.*

THE LIFE AND SERVICES

OF

ARCHBISHOP HUGHES.

THE people of the North were shocked, on the morning of January 4, 1864, to hear of the death of this illustrious prelate, which occurred the evening previous, at half-past eleven o'clock; although the telegraph, two days before, notified them he was dying, still his death took every one by surprise. He was a truly good and able man, as well as a genuine Christian, and was esteemed by men of all religious sects. A better and more patriotic American than he never lived; he was noted for his goodness of heart, undoubted piety, devotion to his faith, ready championship of his church principles, sound common-sense, and liberality of spirit; and all these had made him a moral giant among his people. Upon the breaking out of the present war he proceeded to Europe, commissioned by the Federal authorities to make proper representations to the Catholic sovereigns of the causes and pretexts for the rebellion. On this errand he visited, among others, the Emperor Napoleon, and the result of these interviews will be found on another page, in a letter from the Archbishop to the Hon. Mr. Seward, Secretary of State.

On his return home to the United States, he entered into a brief controversy with the Catholic Bishop of

19

Charleston, S. C., concerning the rebellion, where he took
strong Union grounds, and his reply to the Rebel prelate
was eminently patriotic.   He has built up the Catholic
Church, dignified it, rescued it from debt, and been its
untiring champion in an able manner, and has always
had the warm friendship of many of the most eminent
men of this country, and to them, as well as to the ma-
jority of our countrymen, his death was received with
unfeigned regret.

In the following pages will be found a full and correct
résumé of a life well spent in a Christian manner, doing
good at all times for his fellow-beings, and beloved by
every one his position brought him in contact with.

MOST REV. ARCHBISHOP HUGHES, D. D.

John Hughes, D. D., Catholic Archbishop of New
York, is dead.   In the fulness of ecclesiastical honors,
such as no other prelate ever won and wore in America,
the Archbishop has been gathered to his fathers.   On
January 3d, 1864, at half-past eleven o'clock precisely, he
expired.   In his own terse language, he died "believing
in the truth of the doctrines taught by the Holy Catholic
church as firmly as he did in his own existence."   Nay,
more, he has written : "I believe that, as containing the
fulness of Divine revelation, it is the only true church on
the earth, although many true Catholic doctrines are found
floating about as opinions in the religious atmosphere of
Protestantism.   This is my profession of faith, of the sin-
cerity of which the Almighty is my witness."   A true
Christian died when the breath left the body of the revered
and lamented Catholic Archbishop of New York.

HIS BIRTH, PARENTAGE, ETC.

Archbishop Hughes was born in the town of Clogher, Tyrone county, Ireland, in the latter part of the year 1798. He was therefore about sixty-five years of age at the time of his death. He was the son of a small but respectable farmer, who left his native land for the New World in 1817. He was followed thither by his son, who commenced his career in this country as a florist, having been placed for that purpose with a noted gardener of New York.

HE GOES TO ST. MARY'S THEOLOGICAL SEMINARY, EMMETTSBURG, MARYLAND.

Possessing superior intellectual abilities, his mind and ambition could not rest content with the humble and limited sphere in which he found himself placed, and as soon as he had completed his engagement with his employer he sought and obtained admission into the Catholic Theological Seminary of Mount St. Mary's, at Emmettsburg, Maryland. Speaking of this period of his life, the Archbishop, in a speech delivered in Dublin during one of his last visits to the old country, remarked :

"I was borne westward to another country beyond the Atlantic Ocean. In that country I had an opportunity of improving my education, for legislation there had not attempted to monopolize and appropriate to itself the key of knowledge ; and there, although a Roman Catholic, I was made a freeman and an American citizen long before the Catholic Emancipation act was passed by the British Parliament."

HE BECOMES A TEACHER IN THE SEMINARY.

Young Hughes had devoted himself so assiduously to study during the time he could spare from his floricultural duties that it was not long after he entered the St. Mary's Theological Seminary that his superior qualifications attracted the notice of the principals, and he was elevated to the position of teacher. This position he filled with great credit, and it was from this field of usefulness he was called to another, and he was

ORDAINED AS PRIEST IN PHILADELPHIA.

In the year 1825 Mr. Hughes was offered and accepted the position of priest of a parish in Philadelphia. His good work there, and the early but high development of talent he displayed, his firm, courageous and intelligent conduct in behalf of the religion to which he had devoted himself, his fortunes and his life, excited the apprehensions of some of the most distinguished divines of the Protestant persuasions, and a controversy ensued between Hughes and one of the most prominent clergymen of the opposing sects.

HE IS CHALLENGED BY A PRESBYTERIAN CLERGYMAN.

In 1830 the Rev. Jacob Breckenridge, of the Presbyterian church, proposed to discuss, through the columns of the newspapers, the following question:—"Is the Protestant religion the religion of Christ?" The Protestant divine is represented to have been then in the strength and vigor of his powers. But, notwithstanding this, Hughes accepted the challenge and entered into the discussion with the freshness of a youthful enthusiast. His ability as a sound theological thinker, and his industry and intelligence in searching the mystic authorities and in presenting the then almost hidden lights in our country of Catholicism, won for him the distinction of commanding the respect of his venerable and learned antagonist. In 1834 an oral discussion took place between the same disputants on the question:—"Is the Roman Catholic religion, in any or in all its principles and doctrines, inimical to civil or religious liberty?" And so prominent a share of public attention did these discussions elicit that a large volume has been published, containing full reports of them, and are to be found in the libraries of eminent theologians in this as well as the old country.

HE FOUNDS ST. JOHN'S CHURCH, PHILA-DELPHIA.

In 1832 Dr. Hughes founded the Catholic St. John's church in Philadelphia, and remained its pastor several years. The church flourished under his auspices, and even the persecution of the Catholics and the destruction of St. Augustine in the lamentable riots in Philadelphia, in 1844, did not cause the faith of his followers to falter, nor that church itself to remain forever in crumbling ruins, a monument to the desperation of bigotry.

HE IS APPOINTED COADJUTOR OF BISHOP DUBOIS IN NEW YORK.

In 1837 it became necessary to furnish some assistance to Bishop Dubois, of the New York diocese, who had become infirm from the advance of years and protracted devotion to apostolic duties, and the Holy See appointed Dr. Hughes as his coadjutor. He was consecrated in New York on the 9th of January, 1838, and about two weeks subsequently Bishop Dubois was attacked by paralysis, from which he never recovered.

HE IS APPOINTED ADMINISTRATOR AND BISHOP OF THE DIOCESE.

In the following year the Pope appointed Dr. Hughes administrator of the diocese, and he remained entirely uncontrolled in its government. About this time he visited France, Austria and Italy to obtain pecuniary aid for his diocese, and, having succeeded, returned to this country and applied himself to the cause of Catholic education, and in 1841 opened St. John's College and established the St. Joseph's Theological Seminary, both at Fordam, N. Y. In 1842 he succeeded Bishop Dubois in the full dignity of bishop.

HIS FIRST MEASURES.

"His first measures," it has been remarked, "were directed to a reform in the tenure of church property, which was then vested in lay trustees—a system that had more than once given rise to scandalous conflicts between the congregations and the Episcopal authority. All the eight churches in the city were heavily in debt, and five were bankrupt and on the point of being sold. Bishop Hughes resolved to consolidate the church debts, to remove them from the management of the laymen, and to secure the titles in his own name. In this undertaking he was violently opposed by the trustees, and was only partially successful; but the most pressing debts were paid off, and harmony was eventually restored."

THE PUBLIC SCHOOL QUESTION.

In 1841, he took up the public school question, on the ground that the schools were sectarian, and that it was unjust to tax Catholics for their support. Meetings were held, and an association formed to obtain relief, either by a release of the Catholics from the tax or a change in the system of education. The Common Council was petitioned to designate seven Catholic schools as entitled to participate in the common school fund upon complying with the requirements of the law. This was opposed by the Public School Society and the Methodist and other Protestant clergy. Both parties were heard before the Common Council, Theodore Sedgwick and Hiram Ketchum appearing for the Public School Society, and on a subsequent evening addresses were delivered by Rev. Drs. Biney, Bangs, Reese, Knox and Spring, all of whom were answered by Bishop Hughes in an elaborate speech. The discussion was also continued through the public prints. The petition was not granted, and application was made to the Legislature. A favorable bill passed the Assembly, but was lost in the Senate. The Catholics, by the advice of Bishop Hughes, nominated an independent ticket, and polled so large a vote that it led to some modification of the existing school system. In all this matter Bishop Hughes evinced a resolution and perseverance which commanded the admiration of his adherents and overwhelmed his opponents. In his efforts he was sustained by the then Governor of the State and now Secretary of State of the United States—Hon. W. II. Seward.

REV. JOHN M'CLOSKY APPOINTED HIS COAD-JUTOR.

The first Diocesan Synod of New York was held in August, 1842, and the Bishop, in a pastoral letter dated September 8, enforced its decrees in regard to secret societies and church property. The extent of the diocese induced the Bishop to ask for a coadjutor, and the Rev. John McClosky was appointed.

HE AGAIN VISITS EUROPE.

\ In 1845, Bishop Hughes again visited Europe, for the purpose of securing in aid of the Catholic church in New York the services of the Jesuits, the Christian Brothers and Sisters of Mercy, in which effort he was successful.

OFFERED A SPECIAL MISSION TO MEXICO—HE LECTURES BEFORE CONGRESS.

In the spring of 1846 Bishop Hughes returned to this country. He was then solicited by the late President Polk to accept a special mission to Mexico, the nature of which may be surmised. But he was obliged to decline the complimentary offer. In 1847, at the request of both Houses of Congress, he delivered a lecture in the House of Representatives on "Christianity, the Only Source of Moral, Social and Political Power."

IS RAISED TO THE DIGNITY OF ARCHBISHOP.

His diocese was now divided by the erection of the sees of Albany and Buffalo, and in 1850 New York was raised to the dignity of an archiepiscopal see, and Archbishop Hughes proceeded to Rome to receive the pallium at the hands of the Pope. The first Provincial Council of New York was held in 1854. The Archbishop shortly revisited Rome to be present at the definition of the dogma of the immaculate conception.

DISCUSSION BETWEEN THE ARCHBISHOP AND SENATOR BROOKS.

The trustees of St. Louis church, Buffalo, memorialized the Legislature to pass a bill vesting the titles to all church property in the trustees. Senator Erastus Brooks, of New York, supported the memorial, and in the course of a speech stated that Archbishop Hughes owned property in the city of New York to the amount of five millions. The Archbishop, who had returned from abroad, denied the statement, and attacked both the Senator and the Buffalo trustees. The result was a long and animated discussion in the newspapers. The bill passed, but has since been repealed.

LAYS THE CORNER-STONE OF A NEW CATHEDRAL.

On the 13th of August, 1858, Archbishop Hughes laid the corner-stone of a new Catholic cathedral, to be erected on Fifth avenue. The building is destined to be one of the finest on the continent. The foundations are built; but the further construction of the edifice has been interrupted by the rebellion.

HE GOES TO EUROPE ON A MISSION OF PEACE AND IN FAVOR OF THE UNION—HIS RETURN.

After the breaking out of the rebellion, Archbishop

Hughes, at the instigation of the Government, proceeded to Europe to exert his influence in behalf of the Union cause. On his return (September 26, 1862) he was the recipient of a vote of thanks adopted by both branches of the Common Council of the city of New York, ex-Senator McMurray making the presentation address, as follows :

VOTE OF THANKS TO ARCHBISHOP HUGHES.

Whereas, his Grace John Hughes, Archbishop of the diocese of New York, at a period in the history of our country when further progress in its onward march to greatness was declared arrested, its character for enlightenment, liberality and all the other virtues possessed by the great people and government of the republic were misrepresented and perverted, and the judgment of foreign nations biased against it by the malignant tongues of rebellion, speaking through its agents and emissaries accredited by the rebellious States at almost every court in Christendom, did proceed to Europe, as is believed, in a semi-official capacity, and by his eloquent advocacy of the cause of civil and religious liberty, as guaranteed to all by the constitution and laws of the United States, and his earnest, devoted and patriotic, yet intelligent, persuasive and convincing arguments in behalf of the principles for which the free, liberal and enlightened government of the United States was contending against the most infamous, causeless, and at the same time, gigantic rebellion ever recorded in the history of the world—rendered that government and the country an important, nay, almost invaluable, service, particularly at the courts of France and Rome ; and it is but fitting and proper that, in view of such patriotic services and devotion to the country of his adoption, rendered by one so eminent for his piety, and regarded, in a measure, as being removed by his holy calling from all active participation in the temporal affairs of the world, should be recognized and acknowledged by the authorities of this, the city of his residence, and the scenes of his spiritual ministrations for more than a quarter of a century, and to which, after a limited absence, he is now about to return ; be it, therefore,

Resolved, That the Board of Aldermen of the city of New York, in view of the distinguished and patriotic services rendered by his Grace Archbishop Hughes, in behalf of the general government, while on a visit to Europe, particularly of the courts of France and Rome, do hereby tender him their thanks, and through the members of the Board the thanks of their constituents, the inhabitants of the city of New York.

On receiving engrossed copies of the above the Archbishop replied as follows :—

REPLY OF ARCHBISHOP HUGHES.

HONORED SIR—In accepting these resolutions it is not to be supposed that I am indifferent to the honor conferred upon me by the municipal representatives of the great city of New York. I have, since my return, received some kind receptions, and one or two of a more touching character from the orphans and the children of some of our schools ; but theirs was a welcome to the Archbishop, while yours is a token of regard to me as a citizen and bishop—for I do not consider the one incompatible with the other. My being an Archbishop has not prevented me from excepting the kind testimonial offered to the citizen. In appreciation of this I can only offer a feeble expression of my sentiments. It is true that in going to Europe I went, it may be said, in something of a semi-official character, but not as the bearer of any special message. I was left entirely to my own judgment in the matter, it being kindly supposed that my knowledge of the country, my zeal for its welfare and my own discretion would be sufficient for the purposes that I might labor to accomplish. In France and Italy I was received with unspeakable kindness, partly because I was an archbishop, and partly, no doubt, because I was the Archbishop of the great city of New York. My object was to correct the erroneous impressions that prevailed abroad, and which had been created in regard to the causes of the present civil war—to point out the mutual advantages between this country and European Powers of preserving peaceful relations towards each other. My object was to stem the onward current of fixed prejudices against us, and in which my endeavors have been more or less successful. In France I was received with especial kindness, and had an interview with the Emperor and Empress of an hour and a quarter. The conversation was such as might take place between any two private gentlemen entertaining mutual respect and confidence, and if, at the close of the interview, the Emperor did not understand my views and the condition of affairs in this country, it was not my fault. At Rome it was not necessary that I should enter into any explanations in regard to the voyage which I had undertaken; for its object was sufficiently understood. Rome did not require any explanation; for it is not their habit to interfere with the supreme decision of the governments of other lands on civil matters. If they were not pleased with my advocacy of the cause of the Union, their displeasure was never made known to me, if they entertained any. I do not know that my efforts, after all, had any influence in turning aside any thing like interference in our domestic troubles, or that might tend to increase our embarrassments. All the time I was abroad I did not represent one part of the country more than another, but the whole of it, as I once knew it. I had prominently in view humanity and peace, and there was nothing in my mission inconsistent with my ecclesiastical character. This country, as I knew it, was one; and I hope I shall never be called upon to recognize it as two. Let me thank you for the honor which you, as the representatives of this great city, have paid me, in the resolutions which you have just presented.

HE ADDRESSES HIS OWN CONGREGATION ON THE SAME SUBJECT.

Shortly after the return of the Archbishop he delivered a discourse in St. Patrick's Cathedral, during which, referring to his mission, he said:

I had no message to deliver. Another could have carried the message; but none was committed to me except the message of peace—except the message of explanation—except the message of correcting erroneous ideas—as opportunity might afford me the chance of doing, in the same spirit and to the same end. I have lost no opportunity, according to my discretion, and that was the only qualification connected with my going. I have lost no opportunity to accomplish these ends, to explain what was misunderstood, to inspire, so far as language of mine could have that effect, the spirit of peace and good will unto the people of foreign states towards that one nation to which I exclusively owe allegiance and fidelity. The task was not so easy as some might have anticipated ; its accomplishment has not been so successful as I could have desired. Nevertheless, I trust that, directly or indirectly, my going abroad, in great part for the purpose of aiding the country, has not been altogether without effect.

HE WRITES TO THE SECRETARY OF STATE.

On the 1st of November, 1862, Archbishop Hughes wrote a letter to Mr. Seward, Secretary of State, concerning his European mission, in which he said :

What occurred on the other side I think it would be, at present, improper for me to make public. I am not certain that any word, or act, or influence of mine has had the slightest effect in preventing either England or France from plunging into the unhappy divisions that have threatened the Union of these once prosperous States. On the other hand, I may say that no day—no hour even—was spent in Europe in which I did not, according to opportunity, labor for peace between Europe and America. So far that peace has not been disturbed. But let America be prepared. There is no love for the United States on the other side of the water. Generally speaking, on the other side of the Atlantic the United States are ignored, if not despised ; treated in conversation in the same contemptuous language as we might employ towards the inhabitants of the Sandwich Islands, or Washington Territory, or Vancouver's Island, or the settlement of the Red river, or the Hudson Bay Territory.

*   *   *   *   *   *   * *

From the slight correspondence between us, you can bear me witness that I pleaded in every direction for the preservation of peace, so long as the slightest hope of its preservation remained. When all hope of this kind had passed away, I was for a vigorous prosecution of our melancholy war, so that one side or the other should find itself in the ascendency.

THE NEW YORK BOARD OF SUPERVISORS AND THE ARCHBISHOP.

Not to be outdone in marks of respect to the venerable prelate by the Common Council, the Board of Supervisors of the city of New York presented him with a series of complimentary resolutions, artistically engrossed, in response to which the Archbishop wrote a letter, in which he remarked :

I shall preserve and cherish this testimonial which your honorable body, in the name of your constituents, have been kindly pleased to award me, in view of the services which I may have been able to render abroad on behalf of our beloved, albeit now distracted, country. I cannot say that, except so far as zeal, industry and good intentions are concerned, I have been able to do any thing that could merit this valued token of your approval and encouragement. It is possible that I may have done something, if not to promote good, at least to prevent evil, to the land of my early adoption. This is all that I can say, except that, at home or abroad, I trust I shall ever be a true, loyal Union citizen, praying, as becomes my office, that the bright day which will dawn upon the restitution of this country to its former peace and prosperity may not be far distant.

THE NEW YORK DRAFT RIOTS—THE ARCHBISHOP'S APPEAL TO THE RIOTERS.

Prominent as have been the efforts of the Archbishop, in behalf of the Union cause, there are none more worthy a place on the historic page than his address to the rioters in July last. His very appearance on that occasion inspired reverence and awe. Tottering to a seat, his body feeble with age and physical infirmities, he proceeded to address the once excited throng in words of solemnity and deep feeling. He quieted that agitated mass, and his advice and admonitions entered their hearts and stayed the torrent of exasperation to which the multitude were at first fast giving way. This was his last public act, and it was one that crowns with undying glory a minister of God, whose acts in life were pure and Christian-like, and whose devotion to the cause of the country of his adoption remained with him true and faithful to the latest breath.

Of him it can be said, without exaggeration, that he did more for the cause of the Catholic church in America than any other divine in the country. The Roman historian condensed his eulogium of Augustus by saying that "he found Rome built of brick, but he left it marble." In a spiritual sense, the same remark may be made of Archbishop Hughes. When he was consecrated Bishop of New York, as the successor of Dr. Dubois, Catholicity in this country was in its infancy. The clergymen were few and the churches still fewer and scattered about, miles distant from each other. But in a few years a wonderful change occurred. Churches sprang up in every direction as if by magic, while schools and colleges for the education of youth were founded in various parts of the diocese. In this city alone, through the exertions of His Grace, Catholic schools have been built in nearly every ward, and they are supported by the Catholic congregations in opposition to the common schools established by State legislation. No ecclesiastic of great prominence has passed through so grand and perilous a career with such distinguished honor, unblemished reputation and deserved applause. It has been well said of him that "he wielded the power of a Woolsey with the gentleness and forbearance of a Fenelon." Placed in the embarassing and delicate position of publicly upholding the outward form and inward spirit of the Catholic faith, during times when it was to have no sinecure to be a prelate of the ancient Church of Rome, he succeeded by a rare exercise of courage and wisdom in gaining the respect and admiration of his bitterest opponents. In his death the Catholic church of America has lost its best friend, and as remarked above, the country one of its purest patriots.

HIS LAST MOMENTS

were marked by the calmness and resignation of the true Christian. From eleven o'clock on Saturday night, Jan. 2d, 1864, until one o'clock the next day, Sunday, no great change was noticed in his condition. He remained in the most feeble state, unable scarcely to lift his hand or utter a word louder than a whisper, and that with the utmost difficulty. In the forenoon his attendants succeeded in making him swallow a little nourishment in the shape of some soup, and some of his more hopeful friends supposed from this fact that there was a chance of his holding out for a few days longer. But the hope was most deceptive. About one o'clock on Sunday afternoon he became unconscious, and lay in that condition, with slight intervals of reason, until half-past eleven o'clock on Sunday night, when he breathed his last. He was surrounded at the solemn moment by Bishop McCloskey, of Albany; Bishop Loughlin, of Brooklyn; Rev. Dr. Nelligan, Very Rev. Father Starrs, V. G.; Rev. Francis McNierney, Secretary of the Archbishop; Mother Angela, Superioress of St. Vincent's Hospital, and Mrs. Rodrigues (both sisters of the Archbishop), Drs. James R. Wood and Alonzo Clarke, and a number of clergymen and intimate private friends.

About two hours before his death he was seized with a series of slight spasms, or gentle twitches. Father Starrs stood by his bedside reading prayers for his happy death, and all present joined in the solemn ceremony. At a late hour Bishop McCloskey recited the prayers for the departing spirit, and while the voices of all were repeating, in broken accents, the words of the responses, the soul of the illustrious Archbishop quitted its earthly tenement. He

2

died without the slightest evidence of pain, peaceful, calm and collected. His two sisters stood by his bedside at the awful moment, and one of them, Mother Angela, who has been for many years a sister of charity, performed the melancholy office of closing his eyes.

HIS REMAINS IN STATE—ARRANGEMENTS AND PREPARATIONS FOR THE FUNERAL.

From five o'clock, Tuesday morning, January 4, 1864, until after ten o'clock in the evening, an immense crowd of people—men, women and children—filled Mulberry, Mott and Prince streets, within a radius of three blocks of St. Patrick's Cathedral. The rush to view the remains of the lamented Catholic Archbishop surpassed any thing of the kind that has ever been witnessed in this city. It was estimated that on Tuesday only about fifteen thousand persons visited the cathedral, it not having. been known generally that the remains would be placed there so soon.

The announcement, however, made the fact so public, that there were very few indeed whom it did not reach. The consequence was that the rush was tremendous, and it is believed that not less than one hundred thousand people congregated about the cathedral, some of whom, of course, had to go away without having an opportunity to accomplish the object of their visit—to wit: the seeing of the remains of the first Catholic Archbishop of New York.

The bulk of the visitors was of course composed of Catholics; but there were many of other persuasions, and not a few of them were persons of distinction and mark. A large force of police were on duty around the cathedral; but their services were of little use, as no en-treaties, persuasions, or even physical force, could keep the crowd back. The police did every thing in their power to preserve order; but being unable, for obvious reasons, to exercise the extreme authority of rudely dealing with the people, they could accomplish very little indeed. The crowd, which in general has very little respect for authority, had none whatever in this case. Not even the clergymen themselves could succeed in enforcing upon the people the desirability of proceeding in order, so that all might be gratified by gaining admission to the church. Many priests, accompanied by their friends, were unable to get into the church, and had to return home as they went out.

A force of police were also in the interior of the cathedral, under the direction of Inspector Leonard, who, with Mr. Hart, the sexton, succeeded in conducting matters pretty satisfactorily.

The church in the afternoon was being arranged in a suitable manner for the funeral. The grand altar was draped in mourning, and all the pillars, arches and entrances had already been so clothed. The appearance of the sacred edifice was therefore most imposing and solemn.

THE MUSIC

will be of a splendid character. Mr. Wm. Berge, the accomplished organist of St. Francis Xavier's Church, has the direction, in conjunction with Mr. D. R. Harrison, organist of the cathedral. The choirs of St. Francis Xavier's, the Nativity, St. Anne's, and the Immaculate Conception, all volunteered; so that the array of musical talent will be quite heavy. Mozart's Requiem will be the principal part of the music, and it will be sung with great spirit and force. Other appropriate pieces will likewise be performed.

It is hoped that proper arrangements will be made for the press in the way of tables, chairs, etc., located near the altar. Ex-Sheriff John Kelly is to have charge of the arrangements not religious, and he will no doubt pay proper attention to this hint.

The Rev. Francis McNierney officiates as master of ceremonies.

MEETING OF THE TRUSTEES OF ST. PATRICK'S CATHEDRAL.

SESSION OF THE BOARD OF TRUSTEES OF }
ST. PATRICK'S CATHEDRAL, Jan. 4th, 1864. }

A special meeting of this board was held this evening. Present Messrs. John Kelly, O'Connor, O'Donnell, H. Kelly, McKinley, Lynch, Hegan, Dolan and Carolin.

On motion, Mr. John Kelly was called to the chair, and Mr. Carolin acted as secretary.

The Chairman stated that the meeting had been called for the purpose of taking action in reference to the demise of the late Most Reverend Archbishop Hughes.

It was resolved that a committee be appointed to draw up resolutions expressive of the feelings of the board, and publish the same in such newspapers as they may select. Thereupon Messrs. O'Connor and Carolin were appointed, and to which committee the chairman was added.

It was then resolved that this board form themselves into a Committee of Arrangements for the funeral services on Thursday, 7th instant, and that such committee meet in the session room of the board on Thursday, 7th instant, at eight o'clock A. M.

On motion, adjourned.   JOHN KELLY, Chairman.

D. CAROLIN, Secretary.

RESOLUTIONS.

Resolved, That in the death of the Most Reverend John Hughes, D.D., Archbishop of New York, the Roman Catholic Church laments the loss of an illustrious prelate, whose life was devoted to the promulgation of her faith, and who by his labors extended the benign influence of her sacred teachings.

Resolved, That with grateful recognition we record that from the first moment of his entering upon the duties of his mission in this diocese until the close of his mortal career he upheld with unfaltering arm the banner of our holy church, and zealously promoted the welfare of those confided to his spiritual care and protection. The numerous churches, colleges, seminaries of learning and religious orders, the hospitals and asylums, called into existence by his industry and energy will long remain to perpetuate the memory of his religious zeal and the benevolence of his heart.

Resolved, That we recall with pride the many instances in which our Most Reverend Archbishop stood forth as the champion of our faith, of education and civil and religious liberty ; illustrating in his career the virtues of a pastor attached to his flock, and the ability of a statesman anxious for the welfare of his country.

Exiled in early life from the land of his birth, he deeply sympathized with her sufferings and sorrows, his eloquent and powerful voice being always raised in advocacy of her rights and in indignation against her wrongs. The land of his adoption will cherish the remembrance of his disinterested patriotism and devotion to her interests and honor.

Resolved, That while we bow in humility to the dispensation of the Almighty, who has taken from us our beloved pastor, we are consoled by the reflection that the memory of his virtues and labors will endure to animate those who are to follow him in the great mission of charity, education and of our holy religion, with his spirit of devotion to the advancement of our holy faith and the greater glory of God.

SPECIAL MEETING OF THE BOARD OF ALDERMEN—PREAMBLE AND RESOLUTIONS OF EULOGY AND LAMENT.

SPECIAL SESSION, Jan. 6, 1 P. M.

The Board met pursuant to the following call—

NEW YORK, Jan. 4, 1864.

DAVID T. VALENTINE, Clerk of the Common Council :—

SIR—You will please notify the Board of Aldermen to meet, in special session, in the chamber of the Board, City Hall, on Wednesday, the 6th instant, for the purpose

of giving expression to the grief experienced by the Board
for the death of Archbishop Hughes, and of making the
necessary arrangements for attending the obsequies of the
deceased prelate.

JOHN FOX, First district.
LEWIS R. RYERS, Ninth district.
JOHN McCOOL, Fifth district.
JAMES McMAHON, Fourth district.
JOSEPH SHANNON, Sixth district.
JOHN HARDY, Eleventh district.
PETER MASTERSON, Thirteenth district.
TERENCE FARLEY, Sixteenth district.
JACOB M. LONG, Seventeenth district.
PETER McKNIGHT, Eighth district.
JOHN T. HENRY, Third district.
BERNARD KELLY, Twelfth district.

Present—Aldermen Fox, Jones, the President, McMahon, McCool, Shannon, Chipp, McKnight, Ryers, Jere-
miah, Hardy, Kelly, Masterson, Ottiwell, Farley and
Long.

The Mayor sent in the following respecting the death
of Archbishop Hughes :—

MAYOR'S OFFICE, NEW YORK, Jan. 4, 1864.

TO THE HONORABLE THE COMMON COUNCIL :—

GENTLEMEN—A dispensation of our Heavenly Father,
which will plunge thousands of our fellow citizens in
grief, constrains me to call to your official notice the demise of the illustrious Archbishop Hughes. It is not that
an eloquent and exalted prelate has passed away, but in
his death our country has lost an eminent citizen and
pure patriot. For this we may mingle our tears with
those bound by the most sacred ties to the departed, and
remember, in the words of another great and eloquent
preacher, that "God alone is great." Death has quenched
the fire of his genius, but has no power over his virtues.
Mindful of these and of the distinguished public services
of the deceased, the representatives of the city will, I
am sure, accord to his memory the tribute of their gratitude and respect.

C. GODFREY GUNTHER, Mayor.

Alderman Fox moved that the communication be referred to a special committee of five, whereupon the President appointed Aldermen Fox, McCool, Farley, Long and Shannon.

Alderman Fox presented the following preamble and resolutions, which were listened to with profound attention :—

Whereas, the city of New York has again been visited by the fell destroyer—death has again been among us, and this time has struck down one of our most valued citizens—one of the most remarkable men of his day and generation : John Hughes, Archbishop of New York, has been summoned before the Great Architect of the universe, to account for the use made of the attributes of greatness conferred upon him by the Creator, which have so distinguished him among his fellow-men, and which have so indelibly placed the mark of superiority upon every act of his life : he died on Sunday, the 3d inst., at his residence, in Madison avenue, at the advanced age of sixty-five years ; and whereas, it is manifestly the duty of the Common Council, the representatives of the people of this city—all classes of whom regret the death of the excellent divine, many of whom will mourn his loss as they would the loss of the head of their own household—to give expression to their sorrow for his death, to add their feeble tribute of respect to his memory, and to place on record among the archives of the city their appreciation of the conservative course pursued by him as a public man, his indomitable perseverance in the cause of truth and justice, his exalted virtues and Christian piety, as well as to lend their aid in transmitting to posterity a record of his noble deeds, his good works and his disinterested and invaluable services in behalf of the country of his adoption, at a time when such services as he only could render at the Courts of France and Rome, whither he was sent in a semi-official capacity, by the President of the United States, were of such inestimable value to the nation ; be it, therefore,

Resolved, That in the death of John Hughes, Archbishop of New York, the country is called upon to mourn the loss of a conservative, influential and enlightened citizen; the city of New York has lost a great and good man; the numerous, intelligent and conservative denomination of Christians of which he was the acknowledged head in this country has lost a wise, zealous and indefatigable advocate, counsellor and guide; the religion of which he was such a conscientious and devoted disciple has lost an able and powerful advocate, and its peculiar tenets a learned expounder. His death is a great public calamity; for we look in vain for one in any respect his equal, or one so well qualified to fill the place made vacant by deceased; and, while we deplore his loss, we ask, in all humility, of Him who has thus afflicted us, to raise up in our midst one to fill his place, who shall possess those great qualities that have rendered him so dear to us, so serviceable to his country, and so advantageous to religion and to society.

Resolved, That while we thus give expression to our sense of the loss experienced by our city, our State and our country by the death of Archbishop Hughes, we are not presumptuous enough to suppose that we are adding in any marked degree to the general sorrow, or that our action will materially add to his world-wide fame, and the renown he has acquired in those peaceful triumphs of mind over matter that have characterized every important act of his useful life. Sentiments of profound regret will continue to be entertained and expressed by all classes of our citizens; his memory will remain enriched in the hearts of the inheritors of his faith for all time to come, and his name and fame will be transmitted to posterity, and be revered and hallowed to the remotest generation. The many edifices he has erected and dedicated to the service of the Living God, the homes for the helpless and dependent orphans he has founded, and the institutions of learning he has established, will remain lasting monuments of his disinterestedness and devotion to the cause of religion, of charity, of education, and will continue to retain in grateful remembrance by future generations the name and fame of John Hughes, the first Archbishop of the Diocese of New York.

Resolved, That in his life we recognize a continued succession of deeds of love and adoration for his Divine Master; so in his death we behold the signal for the departure from this sinful world of one who had performed every duty to his God, his country and his fellow-man. The former was a beautiful commentary on the benefits and advantages of our republican form of government, which not only admits of, but assists in, the elevation of its lowest citizens, as it did him, from the humblest walks of life to the highest dignity in the church and in the State, and to the first place in the affections of the people; the latter will inculcate a moral lesson more impressively grand as we contemplate the advantages of endeavoring to imitate the example of Him who was meekness and loveliness personified; Him who has promised dignities and honors, such as the mind of man cannot conceive, to those who, in this life, as did the lamented and venerated deceased, take up their cross and follow him. From our knowledge of the devout and holy life of the deceased prelate, and the hopes of a blessed immortality entertained and cherished by him, it is not presumptuous in us to believe that in his last moments he realized the beatific vision so beautifully and impressively described in the words of "The Dying Christian to his soul"—that

The earth recedes, it disappears,
Heaven opens on my eyes; my ears
    With sounds seraphic ring;
Lend, lend your wings; I mount, I fly;
O! grave, where is thy victory?
O! death, where is thy sting?

Resolved, That out of respect for the memory of the deceased prelate, and in consideration of his private virtues and public services, this Common Council will attend his funeral in a body, with their staffs of office draped in mourning; that they will cause the flags to be displayed at half-mast on the City Hall and the other public buildings on the day set apart for the funeral rites and ceremonies; that the public buildings and offices of the Corporation be closed on that day, and that a special committee of five members from each Board be appointed to make the necessary arrangements for attending the obsequies.

Resolved, That the Clerk of the Common Council is hereby authorized and directed to cause a copy of the foregoing preamble and resolutions to be suitably engrossed, appropriately framed, duly authenticated, and transmitted to the Vicar-General, in order that it may be placed among the archives of the dioceses, there to remain as a slight memento of the esteem and veneration in which the distinguished deceased was held by the municipal authorities of the city of New York; and be it further

Resolved, That as a further mark of respect to the memory of the deceased, the Board do now adjourn.

The President put the question on the adoption of the preamble and all but the last one of the series of resolutions, which were unanimously carried.

Whereupon the President appointed Aldermen Fox, McCool, Farley, Long and Shannon as the special committee on the part of this Board.

The question was then taken on the last resolution, which was also unanimously carried.

D. T. VALENTINE, Clerk.

OBSEQUIES OF ARCHBISHOP HUGHES.

The obsequies of Archbishop Hughes took place on Thursday, January 7th, at St. Patrick's Cathedral, New York, and formed one of the grandest, most imposing and solemn of ceremonies that has ever occurred in New York, or perhaps in any part of the country. A mark of respect, moreover, was paid to the memory of the illustrious prelate which has never been accorded to any other ecclesiastic in the country since the Declaration of Independence. All the public offices were closed, in obedience to the request of the Common Council; the flags on the public buildings were at half mast, and a suspension of business was very general among the Catholic community, while not a few people of different creeds shut up their places of business in honor of a man whom all seem to have held in the highest esteem and affection. The manifestation of respect and good feeling was, indeed, such as we have never witnessed before upon a similar occasion, and was a just and richly deserved tribute to a great and good man.

From an early hour in the morning St. Patrick's Cathedral was the centre of a vast mass of humanity, striving to gain access to the sacred edifice ; but admirable order reigned throughout the whole affair from beginning to end.

DESCRIPTION OF THE INTERIOR.

The interior of the cathedral presented a most solemn, melancholy and impressive appearance. Every thing but the ceiling, windows and portions of the side walls and altar was clothed in mourning. The large pillars—six of which support the arched roofing at either side of the centre aisle—were covered with black cloth, intermingled at the three joints with wreaths of white merino, which contrasted strikingly with the sombre aspect of the remainder of the pillars. It should be remarked here that all the drapery was composed of the finest description of broadcloth and merino, of which hundreds of yards were suspended in various parts of the cathedral. The walls, organ loft, doors, stands, and in fact almost every thing in the edifice, wore a sable aspect, being covered with heavy black cloth and merino. Large bands of white merino relieved the darkness of the organ loft, falling in graceful folds from the rim or edge midway to the centre. A white cross, made of artificial flowers, was placed in the very middle of the loft, with a wreath of white flowers just beneath it. The side walls presented an equally gloomy but grand appearance. Black cloth enveloped them from the commencement of the arches to the floor, with the exception of the half pillars resting against the walls, which were clothed with white merino, spreading out at the capitals into beautiful arches. The magnificent stained glass windows, containing various scriptural representations, formed a pleasant contrast to all this sombreness.

THE ALTAR.

The altar was also dressed in mourning with great taste and elegance. The most costly black cloth concealed the ordinary grandeur of the sanctuary from view, while the candlesticks, turrets and paintings were covered with heavy crape. The draping of the altar proper was relieved by magnificent silver fringing and other light decorations, among which may be mentioned a beautiful white cross. The Archiepiscopal chair, which of course stood vacant during all the ceremonies, from the commencement to the close, and in which the lamented Archbishop so often had sat during life, was naturally an object of the deepest interest. It was beautifully draped in mourning, the arms being fringed with silver lace, the black canopy studded with silver drops, and the edges finished off with white lace.

THE PULPIT.

The pulpit, which is constructed around one of the pillars on the left-hand side of the altar, rising some twenty feet above the floor, presented a strikingly mournful appearance. The spiral stairway was enveloped in black ; the book cushion was encased in black ; the canopy, overtopping it, was clothed in sable garments, while surmounting all was a white crown, edged with heavy corded work. At the back of the pulpit was a studded white cross, about one foot in length.

THE CATAFALQUE.

The catafalque was by far the greatest object of interest of any thing within the cathedral. We have already given a description of this magnificent affair. It is only necessary, therefore, to briefly allude to it, specifying particularly the alterations which were made to it. In general terms it may be said that this catafalque consisted of a rectangular base rising about four feet in height, with an arched canopy resting on four pillars, and covered all over exteriorly with black cloth. Interiorly it was lined with the finest description of white merino. Four black and white plumes surmounted the pillars of the canopy, and a large studded cross crowned the whole. At the head and foot of the catafalque stood three silver candlesticks, with burning candles. On the side of the head of the base was placed a beautiful floral cross, surrounded by a wreath of artificial flowers. At the foot of the base was the archiepiscopal coat of arms, consisting of the keys of St. Peter, a mitre and a cross. Beneath the canopy was

THE COFFIN.

The coffin was a splendid rosewood structure, manufactured in the costliest manner, and containing the remains of the illustrious Archbishop. The corpse was dressed in full pontifical robes. On the head of the deceased was the mitre ; on his body the purple soutan, chasuble, dalmatic, tunic, alb and cincture ; on his feet purple stockings and shoes ; on his hands purple gloves, and on one of his fingers the apostolic ring in which he was consecrated, twenty-six years ago, by Bishop Dubois, assisted by Bishops Kenrick and Fenwick. At the right side of the coffin lay the archiepiscopal cross, and at the left side the crosier. At the head and foot were three floral crosses and a profusion of wreaths. The coffin lay slightly inclined towards the foot, the head being placed nearest the altar. The features of the deceased prelate showed little change since death. The appearance was quite natural, as if, in fact, he were in a profound sleep, rather than in "that sleep that knows no waking."

A solid silver plate upon the lid of the coffin bore the inscription :

MOST REV. JOHN HUGHES, D. D.,
Fourth Bishop, First Archbishop of New York,
DIED JANUARY 3, 1864,
In the Twenty-sixth year of his Episcopate,
In the Sixty-sixth year of his age.

THE CONGREGATION.

The spectacle inside, in other respects, was immensely imposing. Every seat was occupied. The side aisles were jammed, and the galleries were crowded to their utmost capacity, while even the sides of the altar were not altogether devoid of intrusion from people. Hundreds of chairs were arranged on the altar and down the middle aisle for the accommodation of clergymen. All these chairs were filled, and still priests remained unaccommodated. It was estimated that between four and five hundred clergymen, dressed in their sacerdotal robes, were among those who participated in the ceremonies. It would occupy too much space to mention the names of all those present; but we may particularize the following :—Rev. Dr. Cahill, Rev. M. Nicot, Rev. Father Doucet, President of St. John's College; Rev. Fathers Houdon and Snyder, of St. Francis Xavier's College; Rev. Fathers Clowrey and McNulty, of St. Gabriel's Church; Rev. Dr. Cummings, Rev. Father Hecker, and Rev. Edward Lynch, of Yonkers; Rev. Father Keegan, of Brooklyn; Rev. Isidore Daubresse; Rev. Mr. Conway, of Tuam; Rev. Messrs. Reardon, Trainor, Brennan, McClelland, Card, McCloskey, Everett, Preston, Conroy, Nelligan, Moran, Doane, Kelly, O'Reilly, Foly, Hughes, Mignard, Brophy, McQuade, Daly, Brown, Barry, O'Brien, Walsh, Madden, Farrell, Gleeson, Woods, McCarthy and Curran, besides Archdeacon McCarron and other high dignitaries of the church.

The distinguished civilians were numbered by the legion. Thurlow Weed, a Protestant, sat side by side with Mr. John E. Develin, a Catholic. Major-General Sickles made his way to a seat, by the aid of his crutches, and attracted general attention. General McClellan was noticed occupying a modest position in one of the pews, dressed in citizen's clothes. Mayor Gunther occupied the same pew with Comptroller Brennan and other members of the city government. Among the rest we noticed the following:—General Meagher, General Hayes, Judge Daly, Richard O'Gorman, Judge McCunn, Bryan Lawrence, Judge White, Sheriff Lynch, ex-Sheriff Kelly, the officers of the Knights of St. Patrick, deputations from the various conferences of the Society of St. Vincent de Paul, decorated with white sashes and badges, Andrew Carrigan, Daniel Devlin, John Mullally, M. J. O'Donnell, the Common Council in a body, and representatives from various societies.

In one of the front pews of the church sat Mr. Michael Hughes, a venerable, feeble old gentleman, seventy-six years of age, the only brother of the late Archbishop Hughes. He came on from his home in Chambersburg, Pa., to attend the funeral, notwithstanding the fact that his feebleness was so great that he was unable to stand without assistance at each side. In the same pew were two sisters of the deceased prelate—one being. Mother Angela, for many years Superioress of Mount St. Vincent's Convent, and the other Mrs. Rodrigues. Some nephews of the Archbishop, together with a number of Sisters of Charity and Mercy, occupied pews just behind.

THE CHURCH SERVICES.

The services were commenced about ten o'clock, by the chanting of the office for the dead, which was participated in by all the clergymen present, led by the Rev. Christopher Farrell, Assistant Master of Ceremonies, and Rev. Dr. Cummings. This lasted for about half an hour or more, after which commenced the solemn pontifical mass for the dead, or

THE REQUIEM MASS.

This was a solemn and most impressive ceremony. It

began with a grand procession from the sacristy, consisting of a number of acolytes, Rev. Father Christopher Farrell, Assistant Master of Ceremonies; Rev. Francis McNierney, Master of Ceremonies; Rev. Father Quinn, deacon; Rev. Thomas Preston, sub-deacon; Very Rev. William Starrs, Assistant Priest, and Bishop Timon, of Buffalo, as chief celebrant; preceded immediately by Bishops Bayley, of Newark; Loughlin, of Brooklyn; De Goesbriand, of Burlington; Fitzpatrick, of Boston; McFarland, of Hartford; and Wood, of Philadelphia.

It may be stated that in substance or essence the requiem mass does not differ from the ordinary pontifical high mass. It is principally in the exterior pomp and ceremonies that novelties are to be noticed. The services are longer and grander, and in the case here the celebrants were almost the highest in the Catholic Church. It is unnecessary, therefore, to go into details, except on a few points.

Bishop Timon, after bowing before the altar, went to a splendid stool prepared for him at one side, and took off his cape, after which he read from a book held before him the prayer *Exue*, etc. He then washed his hands, put on vestments prepared for him, and prayed, after which he received the mitre and sat down. He next went to the altar, accompanied by the assistants.

After the confession he said the usual prayers, kissed the altar, and returned to his seat, where he took off the mitre. An acolyte again held before him a book, from which he read the *Introit* and said the *Kyrie* alternately with his assistants, the deacon, sub-deacon and other clergymen.

The choir in the meantime sang the *Kyrie*, and at the conclusion of this the Bishop, rising, his head being uncovered, sang *Dominus Vobiscum*, and the Collect. He next sat down with his mitre on, while the sub-deacon chanted the Epistle, without, however, going to the Bishop and receiving his blessing, as is generally the case. The Bishop then read the Epistle himself, with the *Tract* and *Sequentia;* said the *Munda cor meum* and read the Gospel.

About the end of the *Sequentia* the deacon carried the book to the altar and chanted *Munda cor meum.* The sub-deacon at the same time placed himself before the lowest step at the left of the deacon, and, at a signal from the Master of the Ceremonies, read the Gospel, while two acolytes, without candlesticks, stood behind him. The Bishop next sang *Dominus Vobiscum,* read the offertory, washed his hands and went to the altar.

At the sanctus four acolytes came from the sacristy into the sanctuary with four torches and knelt down, in which position they remained until after the communion.

At the elevation the sub-deacon knelt on the lowest step of the altar, at the epistle side, and incensed the Blessed Sacrament.

At the end of the mass the usual blessing was not given; but the deacon sang *Requiescat in pace,* and the Bishop, having said *Placeat tibi,* began reading the Gospel of St. John at the gospel side, received the mitre and proceeded to his seat, still reading. The procession then entered the sacristy to prepare for the absolution.

The Right Rev. JOHN MCCLOSKEY, Bishop of Albany, dressed in his splendid episcopal robes, then ascended the pulpit and delivered the following

FUNERAL ORATION.

"I have fought the good fight; I have finished the course, I have kept the faith; for the rest I know there is laid up for me a crown of justice, which the Just Judge shall render to me." To-day the words of the living would seem to issue forth as if echoed back from the lips

3

of the dead.   It is now when these words I have just
uttered would appear rather as proceeding from the mouth
of the illustrious prelate whose venerated form, still
clothed in all the insignia of his high and sacred office,
lies here before us in blessed dignity and calm repose.
Yes, we fancy we hear him say—" Yes, truly, I have
fought the good fight, I have finished the course, I have
kept the faith; for the rest, there is laid up for me a
crown of justice, which the Just Judge, the Lord, shall
render to me." When these words, beloved brethren,
were first spoken, or rather written, by the great Apostle
of the Gentiles, it was not, as we know, in any spirit of
boastfulness or self-pride; but they were meant as an
earnest expression of the self-consciousness he felt that the
term of his mortal labors was near at hand; that his work
was finished; that his course was run, and that now,
steadfast in the faith, firm in hope, he only awaited the
summons of his Divine Master to call him to his rest.
For year after year he lived to give courage, and strength,
and consolation to the hearts of his friends and fellow-
laborers in the apostleship, and not only to his own heart,
but to the hearts of all his well-beloved spiritual children,
scattered throughout the churches, that when he should
have passed away from earth, when they should look upon
his face or hear his voice no more, they would not yield
themselves up to the immoderate transports of grief or
indulge in tears simply of unavailing sorrow, but that they
would rather be sustained and comforted by that grand
and glorious faith which he had preached, by the remembrance of all his services and all his labors; of how he
had fought and endured and suffered for them; how by all
this and through all this he had won a great reward. So
even is it now.   Our heads, indeed, are bowed down with
sorrow, our hearts are oppressed and overwhelmed with a
mighty load of grief, because our good and great Arch-

bishop is no more. He whom we had loved so dearly, he who was our father and our great benefactor, our guide and trusted friend, he who was our pride and our joy, and who so long stood up among us as a pillar of safety and a tower of strength, he is no more. That voice of eloquence, those inspiring harangues, those lessons of wisdom, those fraternal counsels, those earnest and zealous exhortations which so often delighted our ears, instructed our minds, filled with transports of joy our hearts, all these we shall hear no more. And we have been tempted to yield ourselves up solely to the emotions of our grief, were it not that we do still think we hear him say, " Weep not, dear children; grieve not for me; be comforted by the thought that I have fought the good fight; the work that was given me to accomplish has been finished; I have run the course; I have kept the faith, and I now simply await my crown."

Our loss, indeed, beloved brethren, is great. How great it is, how deeply and sincerely felt, has been made manifest by what has been present before our eyes from the moment that the spirit took its flight from this lower world; by those manifestations of love and gratitude and pious feeling shown by a devoted people, in hundreds and in thousands, day by day, in pressing forward to render their last tribute of respect even to his cold remains, and to look upon his face once more, for the last time. It is not our loss alone—not the loss of a single congregation or single diocese—but it is the loss of the whole Church in this country—a loss felt by every Catholic heart throughout the land; for we do not doubt, we cannot doubt, that when the electric spark carried with its lightning speed the sad tidings of his death throughout the length and breadth of the country it thrilled every heart, especially every Catholic heart, with a pang of anguish. And it filled the hearts even of those who were not of the same Church or faith; it filled their breasts with deep and sincere regret. His fame and name, and services too, were for the whole country, and I may say for the whole Church. He stood forward pre-eminently as the great prelate of the Church in this country; as the stable and heroic champion, as the defender of its principles, as the advocate of its rights, as the jealous guardian of its honor. He was not only a great prelate, but he was a great man—one whose life is marked upon the age in which he lived—one who has made his impress upon every Catholic mind in this country, that time cannot efface. Of such a life, of such a character, of such a history, beloved brethren, it would not be possible for me to speak in any adequate or becoming manner at this solemn and mournful moment. I cannot disguise from myself—I cannot disguise from you—that I would at any time, and most of all at a time like this, be wholly unequal to the task. But on a more fitting opportunity, and in about what is called a month's time, due justice, we cannot doubt, will be given to that character and to that life, and to those heroic deeds and mighty services, by one more fitted and more competent for the task. I am simply to mingle my sympathies with yours—simply to unite with you in paying to our Archbishop, at this time, not only our sincerest admiration and deepest veneration and respect, but also, and still more, the tribute of our heartfelt gratitude and love. It was, beloved brethren—as many of you remember—it was on this day, after the solemn feast of Epiphany, just twenty-six years ago, that that same form that is here before us motionless and cold in death stood up within the sanctuary and before the altar of this cathedral, almost precisely upon the very spot where those remains now are—for this cathedral was not as spacious then as now—stood up in the fulness of health and vigor, in all the freshness and maturity of great intellectual as

well as physical strength and power. He knelt before
the venerable Bishop Dubois, who consecrated on that
day his coadjutor. The holy unction was poured upon
his head, hands of bishops were imposed, solemn prayers
of the Church were recited, the mitre was placed upon
his brow, the ring upon his finger, the crozier within his
hand, and he stood up to take his place then and hence-
forth among the bishops of the Catholic Church.

I well remember that great and imposing scene, con-
trasting so strangely and so mournfully with that which is
now before us. I remember how all eyes were fixed, or
at least all eyes were strained to get a glimpse of the newly
consecrated Bishop; and as they saw that dignified and
manly countenance, as they beheld those features beaming
with the vigor of health and the light of intellect, bearing
the impress of that force of character peculiarly marking
him through his life—that dignified presence, that unal-
terable and unbending will, and yet blending in the same
time with great benignity and suavity—when they marked
the quiet and modest composure, the self-possession of
every look and every gesture of his whole gait and de-
meanor, all hearts were warmed and drawn toward him.
Every pulse within that vast assembly, both of clergymen
and laity, was quickened with a higher beat of hope and
courage. Every breast was filled with joy, and, as it were,
with a new and younger life. Great expectations indeed
had already been formed. We had heard of him before.
We had heard of him as the pastor of St. John's church
at Philadelphia, of his great eloquence as a preacher, of
his powerful argument in discussion, in controversy and
in debate, and we all looked forward with joy and longing
anticipations towards the career upon which he was just
then entering. Those hopes were not disappointed.
Those expectations were more than fully realized. It
was with the greatest reluctance that the then young bishop

had consented to accept the dignity that had been conferred upon him. There was a trying and a delicate task before him. His humility and his modesty shrank from it, and it was only in obedience to the voice of his superior and chief master of the Church that he bowed his head in submission to what he felt and deemed to be the holy will of God. But, having once put his hand to the plough, he never looked back; but rather from that moment all the great energies of his mind, heart, soul and whole being were devoted to the great work before him. He was willing to spend and be spent for Christ; he never thought of himself—he thought only of the Church of which he was a consecrated prelate, of the religion and the interests of the religion which had been intrusted to his keeping—and never did he fail or falter in fidelity to that trust. We all know how soon after he was called to the work regeneration came. The good and venerable Bishop Dubois, bowed down by years, was only too glad to yield his government in such a diocese into younger and stronger hands, and soon we felt and all felt that the reins of administration were held by a masterly and firm, but at the same time a prudent and a skilful grasp. Immediately we saw the evidences everywhere around us of the power of his mind, the wisdom of his judgment and of the devotedness and singleheartedness of his zeal. I will not attempt to enter into any of the details. As I said before, this is not the time or the occasion to attempt to repeat any adequate history of that great man. It is enough for us to remember, because it is within the memory of all, what the diocese of New York, the Catholic Church in the State of New York, and I may say in this country, was when he commenced his career as Bishop of this great see, and what it was when he laid down his honors at the feet of his Divine Master, and bade us farewell.

Five dioceses where there was but one, clergymen counting by hundreds where they were before numbered by tens; churches, institutions of charity, of religion, of learning, springing up on every side; the whole character of the Catholic people raised to an elevation which he himself occupied; and from the eminence on which he stood himself he seemed to raise up all his people. Great works had been commenced and finished; noble works had also been commenced, but not given him to complete. One of the last acts of his life, as you remember, was the laying of the foundation stone of his noble cathedral. He did not expect, he did not promise himself, the joy and pleasure of living to see its full completion; but he indeed thought to begin it, that he should lay its broad foundation stone, and leave it to a devoted clergy and a loving and generous people to carry it on and build it up, and stand it there as an everlasting and undying monument to his memory. It was not to be expected that a life of such labor would be extended to very many years. He sank under the weight of his cares. He had overtasked, many a time and oft, both his physical and mental powers. Strong and vigorous as they were, in the end they sank. He was in feeble health for the last four or five years of his life; yet his mind was strong, clear and vigorous. Still, he knew his strength was failing—the term of his mortal career was drawing to an end. When the announcement was made to him that his disease had reached a crisis and there was no longer hope of life, he received it with the same calmness, courage and composure that he would the announcement of any ordinary piece of intelligence, and immediately prepared. His confessor was sent for; he made his confession with all the simplicity and humility of a child; he received and was fortified by the last sacrament of his Church,

and then he waited calmly and peacefully the summons
of his call. He spent the last day simply in communing
with his own heart and with God. He uttered but
few words; but he gave a loving glance of recognition
to his friends as they came and stood by his bed-side.
He spoke by his look, not by his lips: and after an
illness, painful, indeed, very painful at times, still not
very long, after a brief struggle, he returned his great and
noble spirit.

He died full of years and full of honor, leaving behind
him a record which no prelate of the church in this
country has ever left before, or will ever leave again. And
it can be said, without any invidiousness, that he stood
out prominently and pre-eminently, as we have already
said, as the great prelate of the American Church. He
stood forth as its representative, as its advocate and as its
defender, and all recognized his superior power and great
abilities. As we look now upon that life, through the
softened and gentle lustre which death has already thrown
around it, it seems to rise up—its character to rise up—
even in colossal sublimity. All former prejudices are forgotten, all animosities laid aside, all differences, either of
creed, feeling or opinion—all melt and fade away in that
august, imposing and venerable presence. We think only
of the great prelate and the great man, of his mighty
genius, of his unequalled services to the church; we think
only of the rare endowments of his mind and heart, and
how fully and unreservedly they were devoted to the
cause of his Divine Master. If I may be permitted to say
it, there was one thing that distinguished our great Archbishop most particularly: it was his singular force and
clearness and vigor of intellect, his strength of will and his
firmness of presence. He was a stranger to fear, and his
heart was full of undaunted courage, and in the presence
of difficulties and dangers his energies seemed to be only

aroused to greater strength and higher exercise. He never quailed before the presence of any danger or difficulty or trial. Not that he trusted only and solely in himself. He trusted in his cause, and he trusted in that God to whose service he was pledged, and devoted his entire being. With these rare endowments of mind he combined also the gentler and more captivating qualities of heart. He was the kindest of fathers; he was the most faithful of friends. His heart was full of tenderness for the poor and the oppressed. It was full, too, of genial warmth and sunshine. If there appeared at times to be an occasional tinge of severity belonging to his character, it was not the natural habit of the man. The genuine impulses and feelings of his heart were all of kindness and of gentleness. He despised every thing that was mean and little. He could never stoop to any low trickery. He was candid, honest and straightforward in all his dealings with men. He was unselfish and disinterested in every thing that he did for the church, and in every thing he undertook for the cause of his people—in any service he rendered, either to religion or humanity.

We have this abiding conviction, that if ever there was a man who in the whole history and character of his life impressed upon us the sentiment and the conviction that he had been raised up by God—chosen as the instrument to do an appointed work, and strengthened by His grace and supported by His arm for the accomplishment of that work for which he had been chosen and appointed—that man was Archbishop Hughes. He was from the beginning until death clearly and plainly an instrument in the hands of God, and as such he felt most happy, and as such he lived, and as such he died. It is for us, beloved brethren, now to pay the last debt of affection, which is to pray for the repose of his soul. We do not claim for him or for any man, however exalted may be

his position in the Church, exemption from human frailty
and human infirmity.   He departed from this world, as
we have said, strengthened and prepared by the sacra-
ments of the Church, by a life of faithful toil and sincere
and unostentatious piety, by a heart devoted to his work ;
but still, if through human frailty there should yet remain some stain upon that great soul to be expiated,
washed away before it shall be so pure and undefiled as
to be made worthy to enter into the presence of God, oh,
let us give all the earnest faith of our hearts to prayer !
It is our beautiful and consoling belief that, though parted
in the body, our spirits are still united, and that we may
still love him, and still pray for him—aye, even perhaps
be able to aid him by our poor but humble and earnest
prayers.   Bishops, then, fellow-prelates with him in the
Church of God, we who have toiled and labored by his
side, we who knew him so well, who were so often assisted by his counsel and aided by his wisdom, let us
pray.   Priests of the sanctuary upon whom he has laid
his venerated hand, to whom he has been a light and a
guide and a source of joy, and a source of comfort and
pride, do you pray for him.   Holy virgins of the Church
of God, followers of Jesus Christ, do you pray for him.
Little ones, fatherless and motherless, he who was your
loving parent and generous benefactor, pray for him.
Catholics, one and all, rich and poor, high and low, of
every rank and every condition, you owe him a debt of
gratitude you never can repay.   At least, oh, pray for
him.   In a moment more you will bid adieu, even to
what here remains of him.   In a moment more, with his
mitre on his head, clothed in all the insignia of his high
office, he will go, as it were, in the solemn procession,
bidding you all adieu ; go to take his place with the prelates who were before him, who, beneath the pavement
of this venerable cathedral, sleep the sleep of death.   He

will go, and perchance the prayers of the Church will surround him, and, as the tones of that solemn dirge and of those touching prayers resound beneath these vaults, we still will fancy that we hear, in sweet responsive tones commingling with them and lingering still behind, "I have fought the good fight, I have run my course, I have kept the faith, and now go to receive my crown."

This funeral oration, which was delivered with all the power and grace of a finished orator, was most affecting. Many of the clergymen were melted to tears by this allusion to themselves. The female portion of the congregation wept in audible tones, while many strong men of the world were not indifferent to the affecting scene.

THE ABSOLUTION AFTER MASS.

After the funeral oration the solemn ceremony of "the absolution after mass" took place. Four chairs were placed about the catafalque, one at each corner, and the Bishop's faldstool was brought to the head of it. A solemn procession, in the following order, then issued from the sacristy:

1—Two acolytes, with lighted candles.

2—Two acolytes, one with the censer and boat, and the . other with the holy-water vase.

3—The sub-deacon, carrying the cross, between two acolytes, with candlesticks containing lighted tapers.

4—Several clergymen, two by two.

5—The deacon and the assistant priest, the former at the left of the latter.

6—Bishops McCloskey, Bayley, Loughlin and De Goesbriand.

7—Bishop Timon, between Vicar-General Starrs and Father Quinn.

8—The acolytes in waiting on Bishop Timon.

On reaching the catafalque, Bishop Timon, Father Starrs and Quinn, together with the two acolytes, bearing the holy water vase and censer, stopped at the head;

Bishop McCloskey sat at the right-head corner, and Bishop
Loughlin at the left-head corner; Bishop De Goesbriand
sat at the right-foot corner, and Bishop Bayley at the left-
foot corner. After all were in their proper positions,
Bishop Timon read a prayer, beginning *Non intres*, and
all the clergymen chanted the response, *Subvenite.*

Bishop McCloskey, the prelate first in dignity, attended
by Father McNierney, Master of Ceremonies, put incense
into the censer, blessed it, and, attended by Very Rev.
Dr. Conroy, of Albany, made a circuit of the catafalque
three times, sprinkling it thrice at each corner with holy
water and incensing it in the same manner, reciting the
prayer, *Et ne nos Inducas*, and the verses and prayer as in
the Roman pontifical.

Bishop Bayley next made a circuit three times, in the
same manner as Bishop McCloskey, attended by Fathers
Moran and Doane.

The circuit was made subsequently by Bishops Lough-
lin and De Goesbriand, attended respectively by Fathers
O'Rielly and George McCloskey and Fathers Foley and
Hughes.

Last of all, Bishop Timon performed the same ceremony
as the other prelates, and the *Libera* was chanted
solemnly.

This closed the religious ceremonies and offices for the
dead.

THE REMOVAL OF THE REMAINS.

The removal of the remains was the next part of the
proceedings. Previous to this Father McNierney ad-
dressed the congregation for the purpose of requesting
that at the removal of the remains no one should leave
the church or enter the vault except the prelates, chap-
lains and some members of the family. The undertakers
then approached the catafalque and placed all the floral

wreaths and roses in the coffin. Six clergymen then placed the coffin on their shoulders, and, while the clergymen and choir chanted a solemn dirge, the remains were conveyed in mournful procession through the church, while the entire congregation stood gazing earnestly for the last time at the face of the Archbishop, which appeared distinctly above the head of the coffin, calm and peaceful in the eternal sleep of death. There was a sadness and a quiet solemnity in it that struck the vast congregation with sorrow and awe. The feelings of all were strung to the highest pitch, and many a sob and subdued groan was heard in the midst of the solemn stillness.

The coffin was borne outside the church, where the remains were placed in a vault at the right-hand side of the cathedral—only temporarily, however, as it is intended to inter them shortly in some other place.

It is worthy of remark that the Archbishop, some few years ago, requested Mr. M. J. O'Donnell, of New York, a well-known Catholic teacher, to accompany him to Calvery Cemetery, where his Grace selected a spot, near the mortuary chapel, as the last place of repose for his body on this earth. The fact is not generally known ; but we give it now on the authority of Mr. O'Donnell, who accompanied the venerated prelate on that occasion, when, perhaps, the spirit of prophecy was upon him. Thus it seems that the wish of the Archbishop was not only to consecrate a cemetery for the Catholic dead of his archdiocese, but to be there buried himself, among those whom in many long years he had taught, confirmed and ordained. Further, we are empowered to say he expressed the intention years ago that not only should his own ashes repose in that ground, but that the bones of his father and mother, now buried in Chambersburg, Pa., should also be brought thence and interred with him. This, as we are informed, was one of the chief wishes of the illustrious deceased. However this may be, the remains were yesterday laid, as stated above, in one of the vaults of the cathedral, and the usual services for the dead were read over them. After this ceremony the procession re-entered the church, while the clergymen chanted the solemn words of the *De Profundis*.

This ended the religious ceremonies. The bishops and their assistants, accompanied by the priests, re-entered the sacristy, disrobed and separated.

THE MUSIC.

A word about the music will not be out of place in this connection. It was under the direction of Mr. William Berge, the organist of St. Francis Xavier's church, but only a few of the artists who volunteered their services, had an opportunity of singing. The performance was not, therefore, on so grand a scale as was anticipated. The principal part was Mozart's Requiem, which was sung in the following order :—*Kyne Elieson*, solo and chorus ; *Dies Irae*, chorus ; *Tu Merum*, bass solo and quartette ; *Lacrymoso Christe*, duett for soprano, solo and chorus ; *O Jesu Me Deus Pastor*, solo and full chorus; *Sanctus*, full chorus ; *Benedictus*, trio for soprano, tenor and basso ; *Agnus Dei*, trio, chorus, and soprano solo. All these pieces were rendered with spirit. Among the artists who sang were Messrs. R. Gonzales, director of St. Anne's church, Wernecke, Hubner, Schwikardi and G. Schmidt.

THE PERSONS INVITED.

The following were the delegations and persons invited by the trustees of St. Patrick's Cathedral to attend the funeral services of the Archbishop :—

	Number of Persons.	Number of Pews.
Family of deceased	—	—
Sisters of religious orders	25	4
President of the United States and Cabinet	12	2
Governor of State of New York and staff	6	1
Foreign dignitaries	25	4
Judiciary	25	4
Members of the Legislature	25	4
Mayor and officers	12	2
Mayor and Common Council	40	6
Board of Supervisors	12	2
Board of Education	44	7
Heads of departments	25	4
Commissioners of Charities and Corrections	4	1
Dissenting clergymen	25	4
General John A. Dix and staff	12	2
General Hays and staff	12	2
Army and Navy officers	25	4
Delegations from medical societies	25	4
Representatives of Jesuit colleges	18	3
Delegations of St. Vincent de Paul Society	24	4
Distinguished Catholics	40	6
Distinguished Protestants	40	6
Strangers from abroad	50	8

THE SCENES OUTSIDE.

If the cathedral itself was crowded, what can be said of the streets? Thousands and tens of thousands were there assembled, each individual vainly striving to precede his neighbor in a general anxiety to take the "last fond look" at the face of the cherished dead. The Catholic children of every race and every land were there represented. Every street and avenue of the vast city became as it were a tributary to the vast river of life that went up and flowed on to the first Catholic church of the metropolis, to see a "dead man carried out."

All of these, however, knew well that, though the solemn parting of the soul is common enough, on this occasion there was one borne to his long home who, like Jacob of old, had blessings abundant to confer upon his children from every region and from every clime. The father of the faithful himself, he never forgot his equally faithful children while living; and now, though dead, the common thought was "yet shall his memory live among the thousands who have learned to honor and revere his name."

The pressure on the four sides of the church by the thousand seeking entrance was really tremendous. There could not have been less than one hundred thousand persons scattered about among the streets adjacent to the cathedral. From daylight until the hour the sacred services commenced there was one continual stream of life flowing in from all parts of the city proper, as well as from Williamsburg, Brooklyn, Hoboken and Jersey. At ten o'clock the assemblage was so large that ropes had to be stretched across the streets, at the front as well as the rear entrances, to prevent an overwhelming rush into the cathedral itself. The barriers, and even the policemen themselves, were, notwithstanding, of little or no use. Such a determined massing of people as resolved to find admission, and such unanimity in the fervor of public feeling under all circumstances, excelled every demonstration of the kind ever before seen in New York.

The groceries and liquor stores in the vicinity of the cathedral were all closed, and everywhere was found an expression of true grief among the people, and an earnest blessing on the remains of the dead.

The press of people on all sides was really tremendous. The services of the police were invaluable; but, as was said before, they could not prevent the immense pressure of the surging crowd towards the gates of the church.

Every house in the immediate neighborhood was crammed to excess. The very roofs were covered with people, all of whom were anxious to see the last remains of the reverend Archbishop. The general idea seemed to be that the remains would be carried to Calvary Cemetery; but this idea was soon cast to the winds, at least for the time being, by a few words from the Bishop who delivered the sermon.

It is almost impossible to describe the excitement and agitation of the people outside. They could not get in, do what they would.

Time and space would fail us to attempt a description of the various dodges to which people had to resort to get into the churchyard. Several persons, at the expense of their necks and breeches, climbed over the walls and leaped on the ground beneath. There were many scenes like this to be seen during the morning. Several of these aspiring gentlemen were summarily drawn down by the police, and their flights of imagination as well as of ambition brought suddenly to the ground. It may briefly be said that such earnest enthusiasm and true devotion to the departed have rarely if ever been seen; and it may well be added that the expressed admiration for the deceased Archbishop was not confined to the people of his own communion. Catholic and Protestant mingled together, and struggled for the first place to view his remains; their tears were freely mingled together as for a common loss, and when the remains were borne outside of the walls of the cathedral, there was no sound to be heard but a common expression of love and sympathy for the dead.

4

THE PROCESSION OF THE CORPSE.

The procession of the corpse from the cathedral was about the most touching portion of the day.

Amid the solemn tones of the organ, the voices of the priests, and the tears of the whole congregation, the coffin containing the remains of the venerable prelate was removed from the centre of the cathedral. It was gently borne down the aisle by faithful priests, and on reaching the open air the thousands collected in the courts of the temple broke out into murmuring prayers, scarcely audible, yet earnestly meant, for the repose of the soul of their faithful and beloved bishop. At this juncture of the services there was scarcely a man or woman whose eyes did not show traces of weeping. As for the latter, they were all in tears. The men bore up as well as they could ; but the women—soft as they are by nature—could not restrain themselves when the last remains of their beloved father were being carried away from their sight for the last time.

No possible description can be given that would convey an adequate idea of the crowd of people. The main entrance of the cathedral and all the surrounding gates were so completely beleaguered that it was impossible for any one to enter into either of these portals. Even priests of the church were rejected because they were not clad in the robes of their order. The policemen who were placed on guard, being slightly dubious as to what duties they had to perform, rejected every one who came near them, with or without authority. A few—very few, we are glad to say—squeezed themselves in on the old pretence that they were reporters, although by this process several real reporters were for a time excluded. For impostors like these there should be no mercy. But, taking every thing into consideration, a hard duty was well performed by the police force detailed at the cathedral on this eventful occasion.

CURIOUS FACTS WORTHY OF NOTE.

The Archbishop during his lifetime had often expressed the wish that he would die on the anniversary of his patron, St. John; and his wish was granted, as last Sunday, the day of his death, was the anniversary of that saint. During his term of archiepiscopacy he ordained one hundred and two priests and consecrated no less than six bishops. On the tenth of March, 1844, he consecrated Right Rev. John McCloskey, Bishop of Albany, who pronounced the funeral oration over his remains. In 1846 he consecrated Bishop Timon, who officiated as chief celebrant at the requiem mass. Bishop Timon is an aged prelate, whose appearance, full of years, was remarked by every one during the ceremony. In 1855 he consecrated Bishop Bayley, of Newark, who was one of the prelates in the grand funeral ceremonial.

The disease of which Archbishop Hughes died was Bright's disease of the kidneys.

THE LATE ARCHBISHOP HUGHES.

The impressive ceremonies with which the mortal remains of the late archbishop were consigned to their resting place, and the reverent multitudes who assisted on the melancholy occasion, marked the day as one not soon to be forgotten. When by the providence of God there is taken from among us a man who has filled so large a space in the public eye, and whose life has been one of such eminent usefulness, we suppose all generous minds will be willing to lay aside, for a little time, the prejudices of creed in a just appreciation of the man. For ourselves, we are Protestants; but if we supposed that Protestantism imposed a bigoted blindness to all the moral excellence which has been nurtured in the more ancient church, we would adjure our Protestantism in favor of manly candor and Christian charity. Intelligent Protestants have no scruple in admitting that the Catholic church rendered important services to society during the turbulence of the middle ages. They must grant that many of the greatest names in arts and arms, in philosophy and letters, have been borne by Catholics. For us, it is a matter of pride, not of apology, that we share in the veneration which the whole world pays to ALFRED, CHARLEMAGNE, and COLUMBUS, to the wise and pure FENELON, the divine DANTE, the sublime genius of MICHAEL ANGELO, and the wonderful eloquence of BOSSUET. Nor can we withhold our admiration from the humble piety of many of the priests; the self-sacrificing zeal of the missionaries; the kindly assiduities of the Sisters of Charity of the Catholic church.

It has been our privilege to listen to the Archbishop, both as an extemporaneous speaker and as a reader of written discourses; but we have always felt greater admiration for his off-hand efforts. These disclose to an occasional hearer more of the real character of the man. They were, indeed, less careful and elaborate, probably less instructive; but they were more racy and impressive. There was a vigor, fervor and heartiness, a fulness, both of matter and of diction, in his impromptu efforts that gave them a zest wanting to his manuscript sermons, though his reading was forcible and emphatic. A powerful off-hand speaker, he was above the affectation of trying to copy the off-hand manner with a manuscript before him. The leading trait both of the archbishop's understanding and of his character was a fervid vigor, and this trait never shone forth with such impressive power as in the most forcible of his extempore addresses. On such occasions he never minced his language; he did not hesitate to use strong epithets; and he poured out his ideas with a boldness, freedom, directness, profusion, and honest warmth which would have done credit to a great secular orator.   He had a force and grasp of understanding which naturally sought solid objects and took hold only of the strong points of an argument.   Fine-spun theories and attenuated reasoning had no attractions for him; and his distinguished usefulness has resulted, in great part, from the practical character of his mind, of which masculine sense was the predominating quality.

As the executive head of his church in this country and the administrator of the affairs of his diocese, Archbishop Hughes has, for many years, exhibited abilities of the very highest order.   Whether we consider the charitable, educational, and ecclesiastical institutions he has founded, and from small beginnings built up to strength and prosperity, or the condition of the church property as he left it compared with its condition when he took it, we must recognize in him the energy, sagacity, vigilance, and promptitude which go to make up a first-rate administrative officer.   The millions of Catholic property in and about New York, have been for many years as well managed, and proportionably as productive, as small private estates under the immediate care of their owners. The archbishop's higher functions have been discharged with equal efficiency and success.   Pastoral labors have been performed, the sick visited and counselled, the poor relieved, the charities of the church administered and its youth instructed, with an assiduity on the part of humble and devoted priests that was kept awake by the constant stimulant of the episcopal example and influence, and guided by his directing mind.

Among the distinguished Americans who have died in our generation, we can call to mind no one whose life, in his own sphere, has been so successful—we ought rather to say, so crowned with the Divine blessing—as that of Archbishop HUGHES. All that he could have aspired for in any part of his life, he attained. Official station, social consideration, personal esteem, and not least, the loving reverence of simple, unlettered minds—all these he enjoyed in full measure. All the charities which he founded grew under his eye to a vigorous maturity ; all his pious enterprises ripened into fruition ; though not full of years, he had filled the measure of his usefulness, and was called away, leaving more hearts touched with genuine sorrow than would mourn over the death of any living American.

THE END.

T. B. PETERSON & BROTHERS' PUBLICATIONS.

THIS CATALOGUE CONTAINS AND

Describes the Most Popular and Best Selling Books in the World.

The Books will also be found to be the Best and Latest Publications by the most Popular and Celebrated Writers in the World. They are also the most Readable and Entertaining Books published.

Suitable for the Parlor, Library, Sitting-Room, Railroad, Camp, Steamboat, Army, or Soldiers' Reading.

PUBLISHED AND FOR SALE BY

T. B. PETERSON & BROTHERS, Philadelphia.

Booksellers and all others will be Supplied at very Low Rates.

Copies of any of Petersons' Publications, or any other work or works Advertised, Published, or Noticed by any one at all, in any place, will be sent by us, Free of Postage, on receipt of Price.

TERMS: To those with whom we have no monthly account, Cash with Order.

MRS. SOUTHWORTH'S WORKS.

The Fatal Marriage. Complete in one or two volumes, paper cover. Price $1.00; or in one vol., cloth, $1.50.

Love's Labor Won. Two vols., paper cover. Price One Dollar; or in one vol., cloth, $1.50.

The Gipsy's Prophecy. Complete in two vols., paper cover. Price $1.00; or in one vol., cloth, $1.50.

Mother-in-Law. Complete in two volumes, paper cover. Price $1.00; or in one vol., cloth, $1.50.

The Lady of the Isle. Complete in two vols., paper cover. Price $1.00; or in one vol., cloth, $1.50.

The Two Sisters. Complete in two volumes, paper cover. Price $1.00; or in one vol., cloth, $1.50.

The Three Beauties. Complete in two vols., paper cover. Price $1.00; or in one vol., cloth, $1.50.

Vivia. The Secret of Power. Two vols., paper cover. Price $1.00; or in one vol., cloth, $1.50.

India. The Pearl of Pearl River. Two volumes, paper cover. Price $1.00; or in cloth, for $1.50.

The Wife's Victory. Two vols., paper cover. Price One Dollar; or in one volume, cloth, for $1.50.

The Lost Heiress. Two volumes, paper cover. Price One Dollar; or in one volume, cloth, for $1.50.

Hickory Hall. By Mrs. Southworth. Price 50 cents.

The Missing Bride. Two volumes, paper cover. Price One Dollar; or in one volume, cloth, for $1.50.

Retribution: A Tale of Passion. Two vols., paper cover. Price $1.00; or in one vol., cloth, $1.50.

The Haunted Homestead. Two vols., paper cover. Price One Dollar; or in one vol., cloth, $1.50.

The Curse of Clifton. Two vols., paper cover. Price One Dollar; or in one volume, cloth, for $1.50.

The Discarded Daughter. Two vols., paper cover. Price One Dollar; or in one vol., cloth, $1.50.

The Deserted Wife. Two volumes, paper cover. Price One Dollar; or in one volume, cloth, for $1.50.

The Jealous Husband. Two volumes, paper cover. Price $1.00; or in one vol., cloth, for $1.50.

The Belle of Washington. Two vols., paper cover. Price One Dollar; or in one vol., cloth, $1.50.

The Initials. A Love Story. Two vols., paper cover. Price One Dollar; or in one vol., cloth, $1.50.

Kate Aylesford. Two vols., paper cover. Price One Dollar; or bound in one vol., cloth, for $1.50.

The Dead Secret. Two volumes, paper cover. Price One Dollar; or bound in one vol., cloth, $1.50.

The Broken Engagement. By Mrs. Southworth. Price 25 cents.

CHARLES DICKENS' WORKS.

ILLUSTRATED OCTAVO EDITION.

Pickwick Papers, ...Cloth, $2.00	David Copperfield, ...Cloth, 2.00
Nicholas Nickleby,.....Cloth, 2.00	Barnaby Rudge, ...Cloth, 2.00
Great Expectations,...Cloth, 2.00	Martin Chuzzlewit,...Cloth, 2.00
Lamplighter's Story,..Cloth, 2.00	Old Curiosity Shop,....Cloth, 2.00
Oliver Twist, ...Cloth, 2.00	Christmas Stories, ...Cloth, 2.00
Bleak House,.............Cloth, 2.00	Dickens' New Stories, ...2.00
Little Dorrit, ...Cloth, 2.00	A Tale of Two Cities, ...2.00
Dombey and Son, ...Cloth, 2.00	American Notes and
Sketches by "Boz,"....Cloth, 2.00	Pic-Nic Papers,........Cloth, 2.00

Price of a set, in Black cloth, in 17 volumes.................................$32.00
  " " Full Law Library style..................... 42.00
  " " Half calf, sprinkled edges. 48.00
  " " Half calf, marbled edges. 50.00
  " " Half calf, antique 60.00
  " " Half calf, full gilt backs, etc............. 60.00

PEOPLE'S DUODECIMO EDITION.

Pickwick Papers, ...Cloth, $1.75	Little Dorrit,..............Cloth, 1.75
Nicholas Nickleby,...Cloth, 1.75	Dombey and Son,......Cloth, 1.75
Great Expectations,...Cloth, 1.75	Christmas Stories......Cloth, 1.75
Lamplighter's Story,..Cloth, 1.75	Sketches by "Boz,"...Cloth, 1.75
David Copperfield, ...Cloth, 1.75	Barnaby Rudge,......Cloth, 1.75
Oliver Twist,.............Cloth, 1.75	Martin Chuzzlewit,..Cloth, 1.75
Bleak House,...........Cloth, 1.75	Old Curiosity Shop,....Cloth, 1.75
A Tale of Two Cities,.....1.75	Dickens' Short Stories,.....1.50
Dickens' New Stories,......1.50	Message from the Sea,......1.50

Price of a set, in Black cloth, in 17 volumes.................................$29.00
  " " Full Law Library style..................... 35.00
  " " Half calf, sprinkled edges................. 42.00
  " " Half calf, marbled edges. 44.00
  " " Half calf, antique. 50.00
  " " Half calf, full gilt backs, etc............. 50.00
  " " Full calf, antique 60.00
  " " Full calf, gilt edges, backs, etc........... 60.00

ILLUSTRATED DUODECIMO EDITION.

Pickwick Papers, ...Cloth, $3.00	Sketches by "Boz,"...Cloth, 3.00
Tale of Two Cities,....Cloth, 3.00	Barnaby Rudge,........Cloth, 3.00
Nicholas Nickleby,....Cloth, 3.00	Martin Chuzzlewit,...Cloth, 3.00
David Copperfield,......Cloth, 3.00	Old Curiosity Shop,...Cloth, 3.00
Oliver Twist,.............Cloth, 3.00	Little Dorrit............Cloth, 3.00
Christmas Stories,......Cloth, 3.00	Dombey and Son........Cloth, 3.00
Bleak House, ...Cloth, 3.00	

Each of the above are complete in two volumes, illustrated.

Great Expectations,...Cloth, 1.75	Dickens' New Stories,........1.75
Lamplighter's Story, ...1.75	Message from the Sea,......1.75

Price of a set, in Thirty volumes, bound in Black cloth, gilt backs.............$45.00
  " " Full Law Library style 55.00
  " " Half calf, antique 90.00
  " " Half calf, full gilt back. 90.00
  " " Full calf, antique 100.00
  " " Full calf, gilt edges, backs, etc...........100.00

CHARLES DICKENS' WORKS.

CHEAP EDITION, PAPER COVER.

This edition is published complete in Twenty-two large octavo volumes, in paper cover, as follows. Price Fifty cents a volume.

Pickwick Papers.
Great Expectations.
A Tale of Two Cities.
New Years' Stories.
Barnaby Rudge.
Old Curiosity Shop.
Little Dorrit.
David Copperfield.
Sketches by "Boz."
Dickens' New Stories.
American Notes.

Oliver Twist.
Lamplighter's Story.
Dombey and Son.
Nicholas Nickleby.
Holiday Stories.
Martin Chuzzlewit.
Bleak House.
Dickens' Short Stories.
Message from the Sea.
Christmas Stories.
Pic-Nic Papers.

LIBRARY OCTAVO EDITION. IN SEVEN VOLUMES.

This edition is in SEVEN very large octavo volumes, with a Portrait on steel of Charles Dickens, and bound in the following various styles.

Price of a set, in Black Cloth, in seven volumes,	....	$14.00
"	"	Scarlet cloth, extra,	.... 16.00
"	"	Law Library style,	.... 17.50
"	"	Half calf, sprinkled edges,	.... 20.00
"	"	Half calf, marbled edges,	.... 21.00
"	"	Half calf, antique,	.... 23.00
"	"	Half calf, full gilt backs, etc.,	.... 25.00

CHARLES LEVER'S WORKS.

Fine Edition, bound separately.

Charles O'Malley, cloth, ...$1.50
Harry Lorrequer, cloth, ... 1.50
Jack Hinton, cloth, ... 1.50
Davenport Dunn, cloth, ... 1.50
Tom Burke of Ours, cloth, 1.50

Arthur O'Leary, cloth, ... 1.50
Con Cregan, cloth 1.50
Knight of Gwynne, cloth,.. 1.50
Valentine Vox, cloth, ... 1.50
Ten Thousand a Year, ... 1.50

CHARLES LEVER'S NOVELS.

All neatly done up in paper covers.

Charles O'Malley,....Price 50 cts.
Harry Lorrequer,..........50 "
Horace Templeton,.........50 "
Tom Burke of Ours,......50 "
Jack Hinton, the Guards-
man, ...50 "

Arthur O'Leary,...............50 cts.
The Knight of Gwynne, 50 "
Kate O'Donoghue,...........50 "
Con Cregan, the Irish
Gil Blas, ...50 "
Davenport Dunn,............50 "

LIBRARY EDITION.

THIS EDITION is complete in FIVE large octavo volumes, containing Charles O'Malley, Harry Lorrequer, Horace Templeton, Tom Burke of Ours, Arthur O'Leary, Jack Hinton the Guardsman, The Knight of Gwynne, Kate O'Donoghue, etc., handsomely printed, and bound in various styles, as follows:

Price of a set in Black cloth,	....	$7.50
"	"	Scarlet cloth,	.... 8.00
"	"	Law Library sheep,	.... 8.75
"	"	Half Calf, sprinkled edges,	.... 12.00
"	"	Half Calf, marbled edges,	.... 12.50
'	"	Half Calf, antique,	.... 15.00

WILKIE COLLINS' GREAT WORKS.

The Dead Secret. One volume, octavo, paper cover. Price fifty cents; or bound in one vol., cloth, for 75 cts.; or a fine 12mo. edition, in two vols., paper cover, in large type, for One Dollar, or in one vol., cloth, for $1.50.

The Crossed Path; or, Basil. Complete in two volumes, paper cover. Price One Dollar; or bound in one volume, cloth, for $1.50.

The Stolen Mask. Price 25 cents.

Hide and Seek. One vol., octavo, paper cover. Price fifty cents; or bound in one vol., cloth, for 75 cents.

After Dark. One vol., octavo, paper cover. Price fifty cents; or bound in one vol., cloth, for 75 cents.

Sights A-foot; or Travels Beyond Railways. One volume, octavo, paper cover. Price 50 cents.

The Yellow Mask. Price 25 cts.

Sister Rose. Price 25 cents.

COOK BOOKS.

Petersons' New Cook Book; or Useful Receipts for the Housewife and the Uninitiated. Full of valuable receipts, all original and never before published, all of which will be found to be very valuable and of daily use. One vol., bound. Price $1.50.

Miss Leslie's New Cookery Book. Being her last new book. One volume, bound. Price $1.50.

Widdifield's New Cook Book; or, Practical Receipts for the Housewife. Cloth. Price $1.25.

Mrs. Hale's New Cook Book. By Mrs. Sarah J. Hale. One volume, bound. Price $1.25.

Miss Leslie's New Receipts for Cooking. Complete in one volume, bound. Price $1.25.

MRS. HALE'S RECEIPTS.

Mrs. Hale's Receipts for the Million. Containing 4545 Receipts. By Mrs. Sarah J. Hale. One vol., 800 pages, strongly bound. Price, $1.50.

MISS LESLIE'S BEHAVIOUR BOOK.

Miss Leslie's Behaviour Book. A complete Guide and Manual for Ladies. Price $1.50.

FRANCATELLI'S FRENCH COOK.

Francatelli's Celebrated French Cook Book. The Modern Cook. A Practical Guide to the Culinary Art, in all its branches; comprising, in addition to English Cookery, the most approved and recherché systems of French, Italian, and German Cookery; adapted as well for the largest establishments, as for the use of private families. By CHARLES ELME FRANCATELLI, pupil to the celebrated CAREME, and late Maitre-d'Hôtel and Chief Cook to her Majesty, the Queen of England. With Sixty-Two Illustrations of various dishes. Reprinted from the last London Edition, carefully revised and considerably enlarged. Complete in one large octavo volume of Six Hundred pages, strongly bound, and printed on the finest double super-calendered paper. Price Three Dollars a copy.

J. A. MAITLAND'S GREAT WORKS.

The Three Cousins. By J. A. Maitland. Two vols., paper. Price $1.00; or in one vol., cloth, $1.50.

The Watchman. Complete in two large vols., paper cover. Price $1.00; or in one vol., cloth, $1.50.

The Wanderer. Complete in two volumes, paper cover. Price $1.00; or in one vol., cloth, for $1.50.

The Diary of an Old Doctor. Two vols., paper cover. Price $1.00; or bound in cloth for $1.50.

The Lawyer's Story. Two volumes, paper cover. Price $1.00; or bound in cloth for $1.50.

Sartaroe. A Tale of Norway. Two vols., paper cover. Price $1.00; or in cloth for $1.50.

MRS. DANIELS' GREAT WORKS.

Marrying for Money. One vol., octavo, paper cover. Price fifty cents; or one vol., cloth, 75 cents.

The Poor Cousin. Price 50 cents.

Kate Walsingham. Price 50 cents.

ALEXANDER DUMAS' WORKS.

Count of Monte-Cristo. By Alexander Dumas. Beautifully illustrated. One volume, cloth, $1.50; or in two volumes, paper cover, for $1.00.

The Conscript. Two vols., paper cover. Price One Dollar; or in one volume, cloth, for $1.50.

Camille; or the Fate of a Coquette. Only correct Translation from the Original French. Two volumes, paper, price $1.00; cloth, $1.50.

The Three Guardsmen. Price 75 cents, in paper cover, or a finer edition in cloth, for $1.50.

Twenty Years After. A Sequel to the "Three Guardsmen." Price 75 cents, in paper cover, or a finer edition, in one volume, cloth, for $1.50.

Bragelonne; the Son of Athos: being the continuation of "Twenty Years After." Price 75 cents, in paper, or a finer edition, in cloth, for $1.50.

The Iron Mask. Being the continuation of the "Three Guardsmen." Two vols., paper cover. Price One Dollar; or in one vol., cloth, $1.50.

Louise La Valliere; or, The Second Series and end of the "Iron Mask." Two volumes, paper cover. Price $1.00, or in one vol., cloth, $1.50.

The Memoirs of a Physician. Beautifully Illustrated. Two vols., paper cover. Price One Dollar; or bound in one volume, cloth, for $1.50.

The Queen's Necklace. A Sequel to the "Memoirs of a Physician." Two vols., paper cover. Price $1.00; or in one vol., cloth, for $1.50.

Six Years Later; or, Taking of the Bastile. A Continuation of "The Queen's Necklace." Two vols., paper cover. Price One Dollar; or in one vol., cloth, for $1.50.

Countess of Charny; or, The Fall of the French Monarchy. Sequel to Six Years Later. Two vols., paper cover. Price One Dollar; or in one volume, cloth, for $1.50.

Andree de Taverney. A Sequel to and continuation of the Countess of Charny. Two volumes, paper $1.00; or in one vol., cloth, for $1.50.

The Chevalier. A Sequel to, and final end of "Andree De Taverney." One vol. Price 75 cents.

The Adventures of a Marquis. Two vols., paper cover. Price 1.00; or in one vol., cloth, for $1.50.

The Forty-Five Guardsmen. Price 75 cents, or a finer edition in one volume, cloth. Price $1.50.

The Iron Hand. Price 75 cents, in paper cover, or a finer edition in one volume, cloth, for $1.50.

Diana of Meridor. Two volumes, paper cover. Price One Dollar; or in one vol., cloth, for $1.50.

Edmond Dantes. Being a Sequel to Dumas' celebrated novel of the "Count of Monte-Cristo." Price 50 cts.

Annette; or, The Lady of the Pearls. A Companion to "Camille." Price 50 cents.

The Fallen Angel. A Story of Love and Life in Paris. One volume. Price 50 cents.

The Man with Five Wives. Complete in one volume. Price 50 cts.

George; or, The Planter of the Isle of France. One volume. Price Fifty cents.

Genevieve; or, The Chevalier of Maison Rouge. One volume. Illustrated. Price 50 cents.

The Mohicans of Paris. 50 cts.

Sketches in France. 50 cents.

Isabel of Bavaria. Price 50 cts.

Felina de Chambure; or, The Female Fiend. Price 50 cents.

The Horrors of Paris. 50 cents.

The Twin Lieutenants. One vol. Price 50 cts.

The Corsican Brothers. 25 cts.

FRANK E. SMEDLEY'S WORKS.

Harry Coverdale's Courtship and Marriage. Two vols., paper. Price $1.00; or cloth, $1.50.

Lorrimer Littlegood. By author of "Frank Fairleigh." Two vols., paper. Price $1.00; or cloth, $1.50.

Frank Fairleigh. One volume, cloth, $1.50; or cheap edition in paper cover, for 75 cents.

Lewis Arundel. One vol., cloth. Price $1.50; or cheap edition in paper cover, for 75 cents.

Fortunes and Misfortunes of Harry Racket Scapegrace. Cloth. Price $1.50; or cheap edition in paper cover, for 50 cents.

Tom Racquet; and His Three Maiden Aunts. Illustrated. 50 cents.

MISS BREMER'S NEW WORKS.

The Father and Daughter. By Fredrika Bremer. Two vols. paper. Price $1.00 ; or cloth, $1.50.

The Four Sisters. Two vols., paper cover. Price One Dollar ; or in one volume, cloth, for $1.50.

The Neighbors. Two vols., paper cover. Price One Dollar ; or in one volume, cloth, for $1.50.

The Home. Two volumes, paper cover. Price One Dollar ; or in one volume, cloth, for $1.50.

Life in the Old World; or, Two Years in Switzerland and Italy. Complete in two large duodecimo volumes, of near 1000 pages. Price $3.00.

GREEN'S WORKS ON GAMBLING.

Gambling Exposed. By J. H. Green, the Reformed Gambler. Two vols., paper cover. Price $1.00 ; or in one volume, cloth, gilt, for $1.50.

The Gambler's Life. Two vols., paper cover. Price One Dollar ; or in one vol., cloth, gilt, for $1.50.

The Secret Band of Brothers. Two volumes, paper cover. Price One Dollar ; or bound in one volume, cloth, for $1.50.

The Reformed Gambler. Two vols., paper. Price One Dollar ; or in one vol., cloth, for $1.50.

MRS. GREY'S NEW BOOKS.

Little Beauty. Two vols., paper cover. Price One Dollar ; or in one volume, cloth, for $1.50.

Cousin Harry. Two vols., paper cover. Price One Dollar ; or in one volume, cloth, for $1.50.

The Flirt. One vol. octavo, paper cover, 50 cents ; or in cloth, for 75 cents.

MRS. GREY'S POPULAR NOVELS.

Price Twenty-Five Cents each.

Gipsy's Daughter.
Lena Cameron.
Belle of the Family.
Sybil Lennard.
Duke and Cousin.
The Little Wife.
Passion & Principle. 50 cents.

The Manœuvring Mother.
The Young Prima Donna.
Alice Seymour.
Baronet's Daughters.
Old Dower House.
Hyacinthe.
Mary Seaham. Price 50 cents.

G. P. R. JAMES'S NEW BOOKS.

The Cavalier. An Historical Romance. With a steel portrait of the author. Two vols., paper cover. Price $1.00 ; or in one vol., cloth, for $1.50.

The Man in Black. Price 50 cts.

Arrah Neil. Price 50 cents.

Lord Montagu's Page. Two volumes, paper cover. Price One Dollar ; or in one vol., cloth, $1.50.

Mary of Burgundy. Price 50 cts.

Eva St. Clair; and other Tales. Price 25 cents.

MISS ELLEN PICKERING'S WORKS.

Price Thirty-Eight Cents each.

Who Shall be Heir?
Merchant's Daughter.
The Secret Foe.
The Expectant.
The Fright.
Quiet Husband.

Ellen Wareham.
Nan Darrel.
Prince and Pedlar.
The Squire.
The Grumbler. 50 cents
Orphan Niece. 50 cents

COINS OF THE WORLD.

Petersons' Complete Coin Book, containing Perfect Fac-Similes of all the various Gold, Silver, and other Metallic Coins, throughout the World, near Two Thousand in all, being the most complete Coin Book in the World, with the United States Mint Value of each Coin under it. Price $1.00.

MISS PARDOE'S WORKS.

The Jealous Wife. By Miss Pardoe. Complete in one large octavo volume. Price Fifty cents.

The Wife's Trials. By Miss Pardoe. Complete in one large octavo volume. Price Fifty cents.

The Rival Beauties. By Miss Pardoe. Complete in one large octavo volume. Price Fifty cents.

Romance of the Harem. By Miss Pardoe. Complete in one large octavo volume. Price Fifty cents.

Confessions of a Pretty Woman. By Miss Pardoe. Complete in one large octavo volume. Price Fifty cents.

Miss Pardoe's Complete Works. *This comprises the whole of the above Five works, and are bound in cloth, gilt, in one large octavo volume. Price* $2.50.

The Adopted Heir. By Miss Pardoe. Two vols., paper. Price $1.00; or in one vol., cloth, for $1.50.

W. H. MAXWELL'S WORKS.

Stories of Waterloo. One of the best books in the English language. One vol. Price Fifty cents.

Brian O'Lynn; or, Luck is Everything. Price 50 cents.

Wild Sports in West. 50 cents.

SAMUEL C. WARREN'S BOOKS.

Ten Thousand a Year. Complete in two volumes, paper cover. Price One Dollar; or a finer edition, in one volume, cloth, for $1.50.

Diary of a Medical Student. By author of "Ten Thousand a Year." Complete in one octavo volume, paper cover. Price 50 cents.

EMERSON BENNETT'S WORKS.

The Border Rover. Fine edition bound in cloth, for $1.50; or Railroad Edition for One Dollar.

Clara Moreland. Fine edition bound in cloth, for $1.50; or Railroad Edition for One Dollar.

The Forged Will. Fine edition bound in cloth, for $1.50; or Railroad Edition for One Dollar.

Ellen Norbury. Fine edition bound in cloth, for $1.50; or Railroad Edition for One Dollar.

Bride of the Wilderness. Fine edition bound in cloth, for $1.50; or Railroad Edition for $1.00.

Kate Clarendon. Fine edition bound in cloth, for $1.50; or Railroad Edition for One Dollar.

Viola. Fine edition, cloth, for $1.50; or Railroad Edition for One Dollar.

Heiress of Bellefonte and Walde-Warren. Price 50 cents.

Pioneer's Daughter; and the Unknown Countess. 50 cents.

DOESTICKS' BOOKS.

Doesticks' Letters. Complete in two vols., paper cover. Price One Dollar; or in one vol., cloth, $1.50.

Plu-ri-bus-tah. Complete in two vols., paper cover. Price One Dollar; or in one vol., cloth, $1.50.

The Elephant Club. Complete in two vols., paper cover. Price $1.00; or in one vol., cloth, $1.50.

Witches of New York. Complete in two vols., paper cover. Price $1.00; or in one vol., cloth, $1.50.

Nothing to Say. Illustrated. Price 50 cents.

DR. HOLLICK'S WORKS.

Dr. Hollick's Anatomy and Physiology; with a large Dissected Plate of the Human Figure. Price $1.25, bound.

Dr. Hollick's Family Physician. A Pocket-Guide for Everybody. Complete in one volume, paper cover. Price 25 cents.

SMOLLETT'S AND FIELDING'S GREAT WORKS.

Peregrine Pickle; and His Adventures. Two vols., octavo. $1.00.

Humphrey Clinker. 50 cents.

Tom Jones. Two volumes. $1.00.

Amelia. One volume. Fifty cents.

Joseph Andrews. Fifty cents.